MEGA MASH-UP

Romans vs. Dinosaurs on Mars

Draw your own adventure!

Nikalas Catlow
Tim Wesson

nosy crow™

An imprint of Candlewick Press

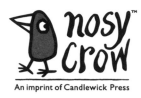

An imprint of Candlewick Press

Copyright © 2011 by Nikalas Catlow and Tim Wesson

First U.S. edition 2011

Library of Congress Cataloging-in-Publication Data is available.

Library of Congress Catalog Card Number pending

ISBN 978-0-7636-5872-4

11 12 13 14 15 16 BVG 10 9 8 7 6 5 4 3 2 1

Printed in Berryville, VA, U.S.A.

This book was typeset in Agenda.
The illustrations were created digitally.

Nosy Crow
an imprint of
Candlewick Press
99 Dover Street
Somerville, Massachusetts 02144

www.nosycrow.com
www.candlewick.com

Your hand

This book needs **YOU!**

What if the ROMANS and DINOSAURS lived on **MARS?** What if a HUGE ASTEROID was about to crash into the planet and **exPLode?** What would they all do? Would they invent something :SPECTACULAR: and then have some FUN AND GAMES? You'll have to finish the illustrations and find out. . . .

Prepare to **LAUGH** while you doodle and SNICKER while you read.

INTRODUCING the Romans of Romasauria!

★ Augustus Astronomus ★

★ Grittus Cementus ★

★ Maximus Victorious ★

★ Ingenius Inventus ★

★ Marcus Linus ★

Introducing the Dinosaurs of Romasauria!

★ Eurekadon ★

★ Caesardon ★

★ Raptor Remedus ★

★ Tiberius Rex ★

★ Clawdius ★

You'll need these. . . .

DRAWING tools

These are the **3** tools that Nikalas and Tim used to create the artwork in this book.

PEN

crayon

felt-tip pen or marker

pencil

crayon

Using different tools helps create great drawings.

texture page

pen zigzags

pencil cross-hatching

crayon rubbing from linoleum floor

crayon rubbing from wood floor

pencil rubbing from wooden door

scribbly pencil

There are lots of ways you can add texture to your artwork. Here are a few examples.

crayon rubbing from floor

pencil dashes

pen circles

DRAWING TIP!
Turn to the back of the book for ideas on stuff you might want to draw in this adventure.

Chapter 1
In the
Beginning

Extend the elevated road.

Two dinosaurs, **Clawdius** and **Caesardon**, are discussing their Roman neighbors. "It's all roads, roads, roads with them," complains Clawdius.

"I know," grumbles Caesardon. "What's wrong with **squelching** through the primordial **swamp** like the rest of us?"

Not far away, Grittus Cementus is laying down paving for another new **ROAD**. "Hurry up! I want to get the lines painted before those **big muddy DINOSAURS** come along!" shouts Marcus Linus.

Other road equipment here

Finish the Romans at work sign.

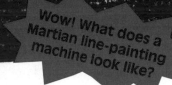

Soon all is ready for a spectacular Rocket Chariot Race. Two chariots are zooming around while the crowd goes crazy! "**GO, Tiberius Rex!**" roar the Dinosaurs. "**Hail, Maximus Victorious!**" chant the Romans. "And what a splendid road!"

Maximus Victorious wins the race!
"Thanks for the trophy and stuff," says the
triumphant Roman. **"HaiL! HaiL! HaiL!"**
chants the crowd.

Show a Dinosaur being thrown into the air.

Show a sandal being thrown into the air.

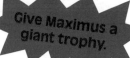

A celebratory feast of **MOON-COW AND FRIES**
is served. The sound of munching can be heard
all over Romasauria. Caesardon lets out a huge
BUUUUURRP. "Manners!" splutters Grittus Cementus,
spraying the table with chewed-up moon-cow.
How gross!

Chapter 2
An Asteroid
is Coming!

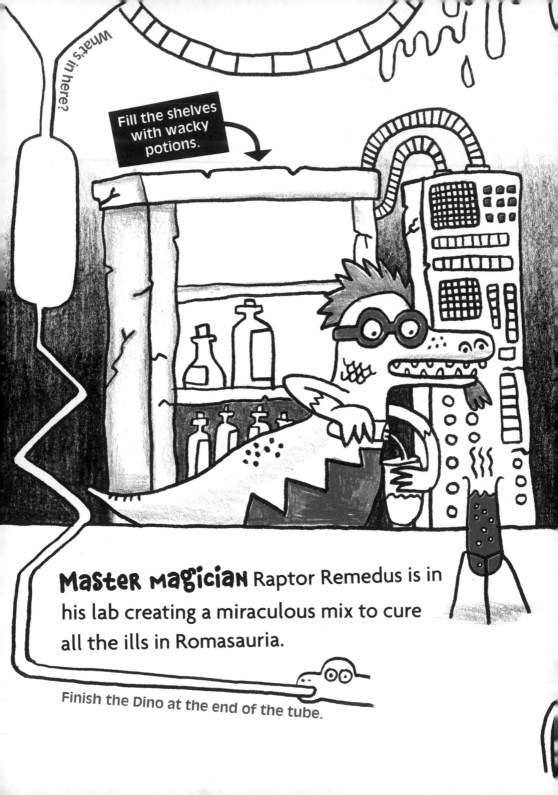

What's in here?

Fill the shelves with wacky potions.

Master magician Raptor Remedus is in his lab creating a miraculous mix to cure all the ills in Romasauria.

Finish the Dino at the end of the tube.

One DROP of the potion gives **Carrotasaurus X-Ray Vision.** "Shall I use my power for good or evil?" he wonders.

Evil thought in here

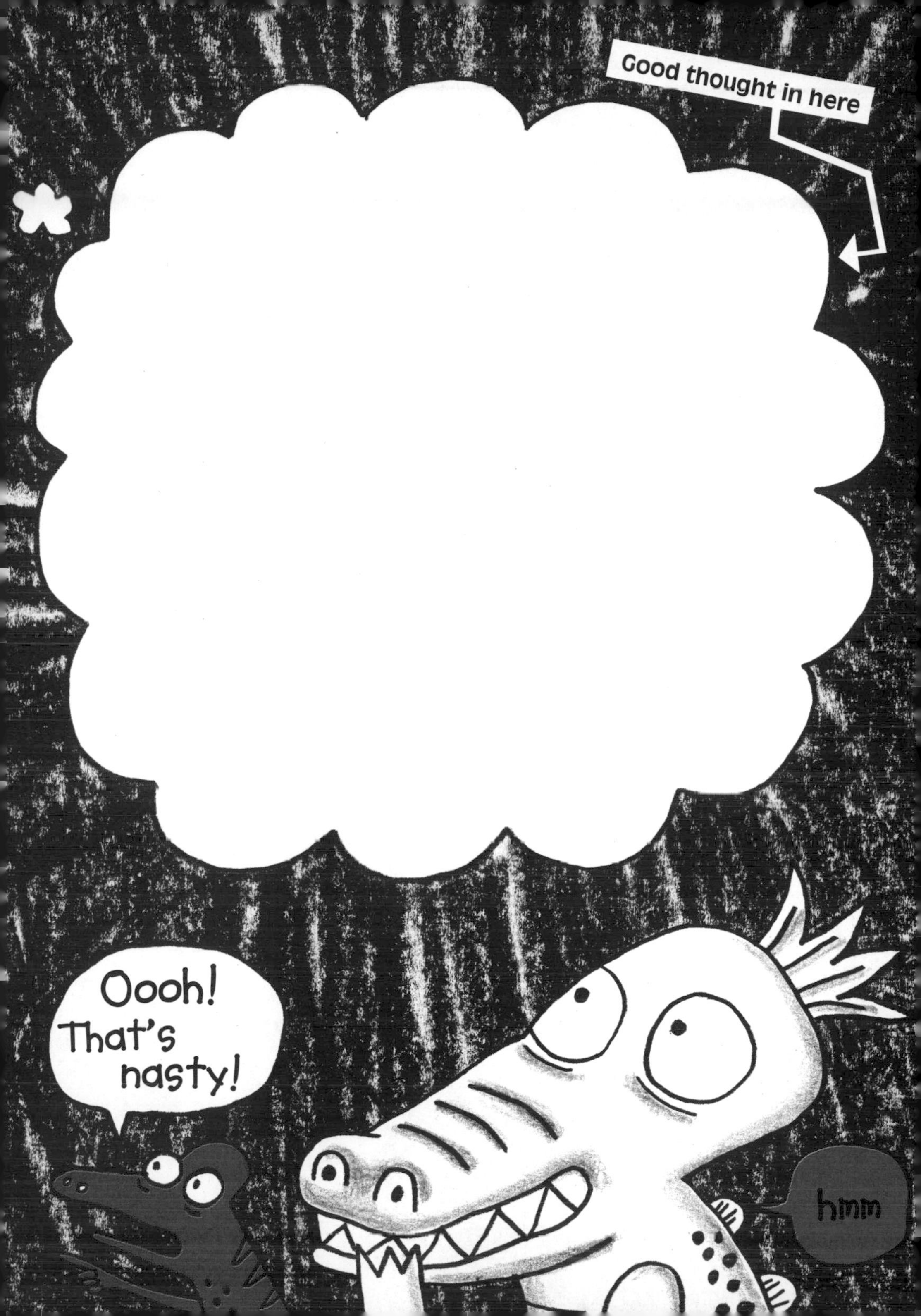
Good thought in here
Oooh! That's nasty!
hmm

Two DROPS give Tinyearus SUPER HEARING. "I can listen to everything that is going on in Romasauria!" he exclaims.

WOW.
What can he hear?

THREE DROPS cure wrinkles and boils.

However, there are side effects.

"Don't worry about those. Er, I don't think they're permanent," says Raptor Remedus.

Cripes!

What color is this Roman with Footheaditis?

What is the clumsy magician saying?

What else has been turned to stone?

FOUR DROPS accidentally fall on a passing Minidon. It is turned rock solid. "OOPS," says Raptor Remedus. "Still, such a power could be useful one day!"

UH-OH! Some other Dinos have been turned to stone!

A perfect opportunity to draw a still life!

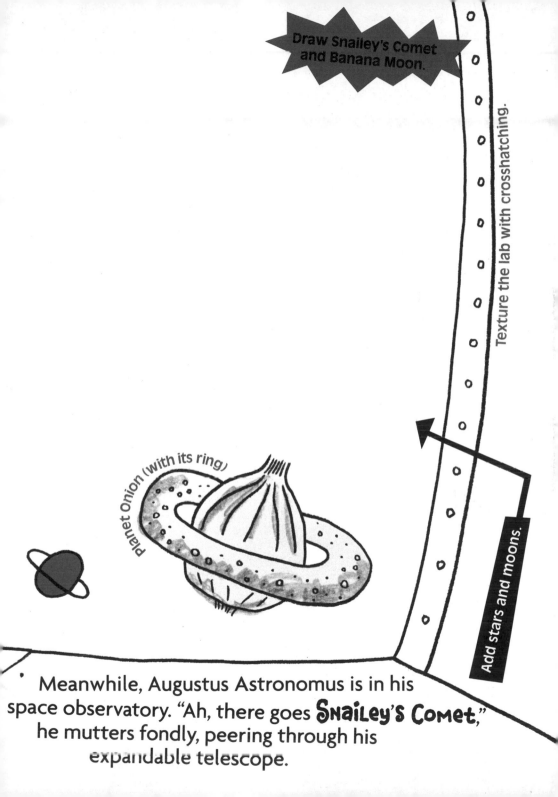

Draw Snailey's Comet and Banana Moon.

Texture the lab with crosshatching.

Planet Onion (with its ring)

Add stars and moons.

Meanwhile, Augustus Astronomus is in his space observatory. "Ah, there goes **SNAILEY'S COMET**," he mutters fondly, peering through his expandable telescope.

SUDDENLY Augustus spots something that nearly blows his sandals off! A massive asteroid is on a collision course with Romasauria. "**BLESS MY TOGA!** It will hit this afternoon!" he exclaims.

Use a crayon to fill in the sky.

Add more planets and stars.

Shade in the observatory.

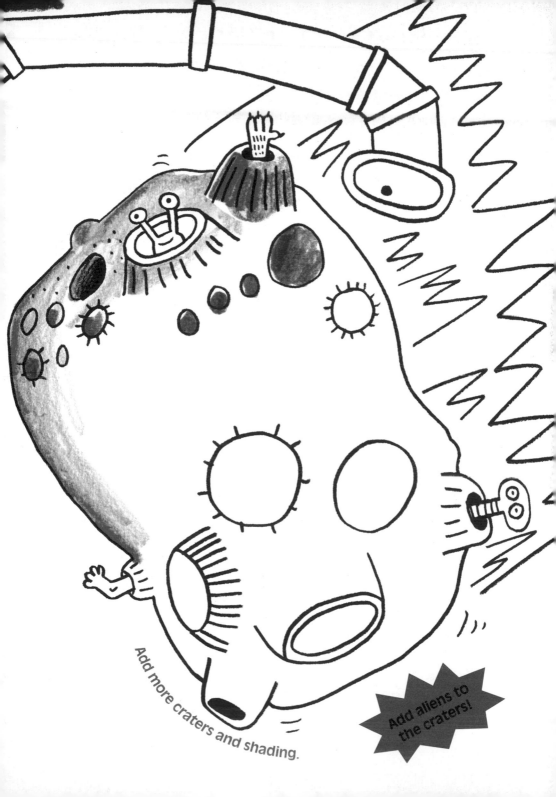

Add more craters and shading.

Add aliens to the craters!

Augustus doesn't waste time. He races up the paved
street to the top of Romasauria, where the great
Horn of Pandaemonius has stood idle for many years.
He blows three long warning **toots** on the horn,
which echo all around the dome.

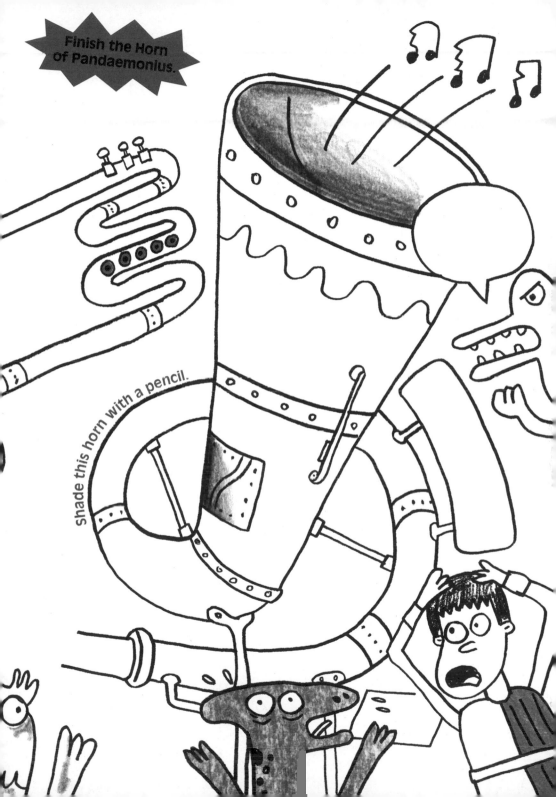

Who else is on the Town Hall steps?

This pillar needs a statue.

The news about the
asteroid travels fast.
There is widespread **Panic** in Romasauria.
"Fear not!" cries Caesardon. "We will think of something.
Er . . . any ideas?"

Is this the end of Romasauria?

Who will save them from **CERTAIN DEATH**?

Will they ever eat moon-cow

and fries again?

Chapter 3

The Roman
way

Ingenius Inventus steps forward. "Stand aside! Coming through!" he announces, dragging a large **WOODEN MACHINE**. What in the name of Romasauria is that? wonders the crowd.

Who's sneaked into the sling?

"It's a catapult," explains Ingenius.

"A really **HEAVY DINOSAUR** climbs into the sling.

Then we pull the lever, the Dinosaur plummets
to the ground, and the machine flings
deadly sandals at the asteroid
and breaks it into a

thousand pieces!"

"**HURRAH**!"

cheer the Romans.

There's no need for that!

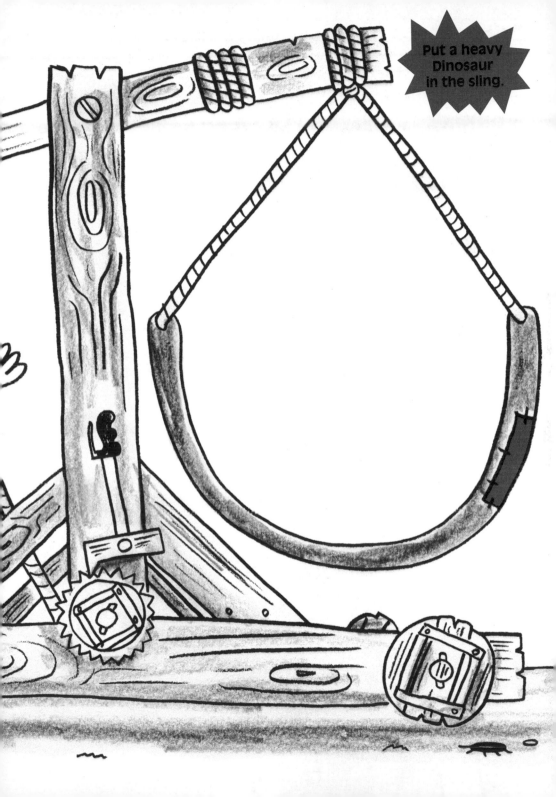

Put a heavy Dinosaur in the sling.

"What did you say about deadly sandals?" asks Caesardon. "The deadly sandals are flung at the asteroid and—" But Ingenius's words are drowned out by the Dinosaurs' **HONKING** laughter. "**Ha ha ha ha ha ha!** That's the funniest thing we've ever heard!"

Help Ingenius explain his idea.

DEADLY SANDAL

What are those smart-aleck Dinosaurs saying?

Draw your own laughing Dinosaur.

The Romans are angry. All eyes turn to Eurekadon, who **WHIPS** the cloth away from an invention of his own. "Ta-da! Friends, Romans, countrymen, I give you the **TORPOODO**! It is Dinosaur dung, squished and baked in the Mars sun. It will save the day!"

Ooh, he looks REALLY mad.

Finish the angry-looking Romans.

Show the huge asteroid coming!

Texture the rock.

"We will form a mighty tower of Dinosaurs, then the smallest one will lob TorPOOdoes at the asteroid, breaking it into a thousand pieces!"

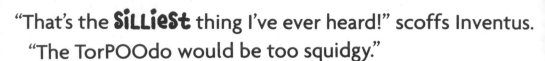

"That's the **SiLLiesT** thing I've ever heard!" scoffs Inventus.
"The TorPOOdo would be too squidgy."
"All right, toga-boy, that's it," snarls Eurekadon.
"Oh, yeah, lizard-face? **You anD whose cenTuRiONS**?"
A fight breaks out. "Eat my deadly sandal!" says Ingenius.
"TorPOOdoes away!" cries Eurekadon.

Add some more fighting sound effects!

POW!

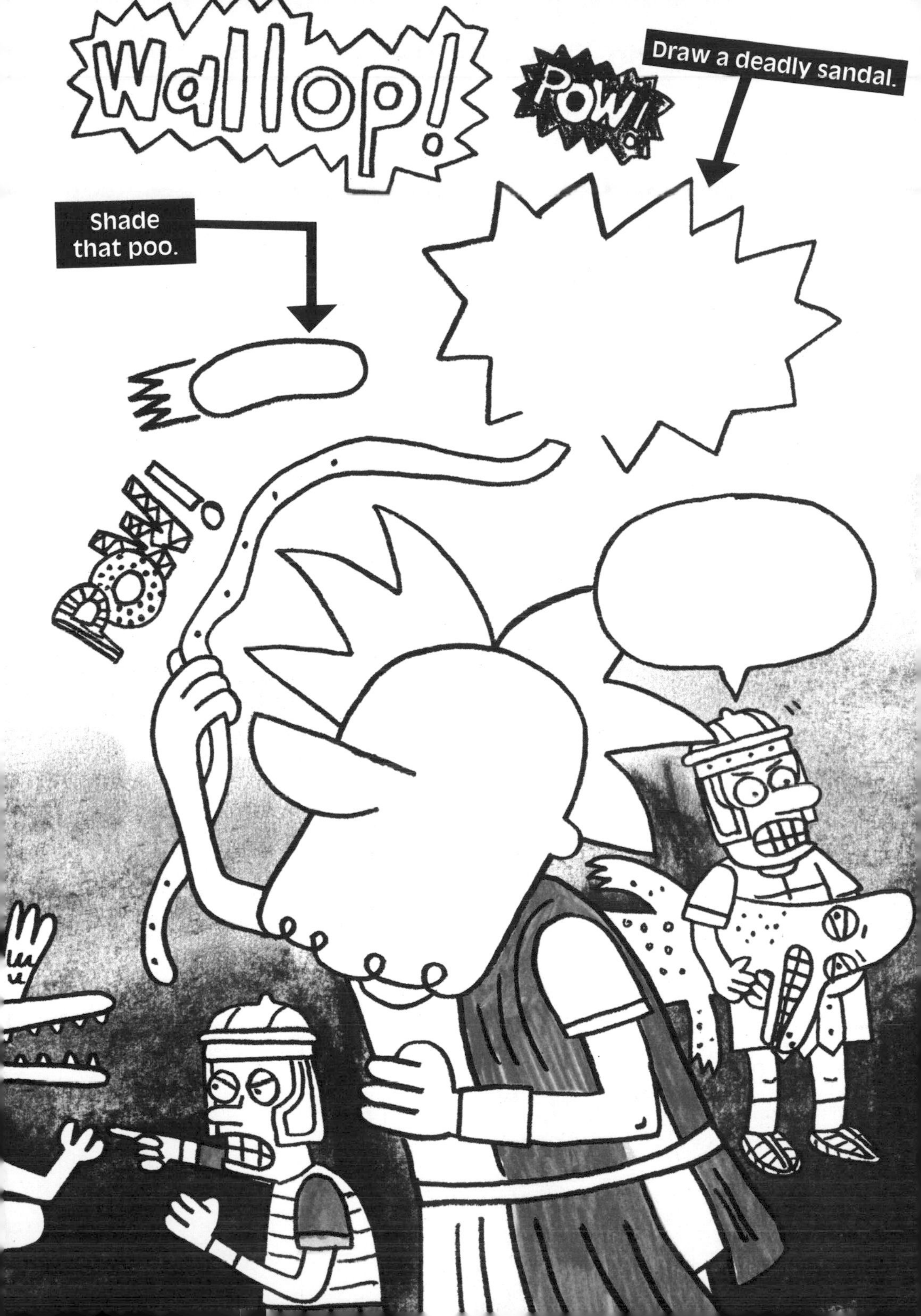
Wallop!
POW!
Draw a deadly sandal.
Shade that poo.
POW!

"Oh, this won't do. Only **MAGIC** can save us now,"
wails Caesardon.
Tinysaurus pushes his way through the crowd.

"Did you say **MAGIC**?"

he splutters. "Raptor Remedus's

MAGIC potion might

just do the trick!"

What's behind
Caesardon's back?

"By Georgeasaurus, that's it!" shouts Clawdius.

"**Fetch the Potion, fast!**" Tinysaurus hotfoots it across Romasauria as fast as his teeny legs will carry him. . . .

What's going on in Crater Park?

scribble texture in the rest of the park.

Chapter 4

The Martian

Magician

There is a small line outside the lab.
"Hey! Wait your turn!" **grumbles** Bulbus Maximus.

"No time for that!" cries Tinysaurus, flashing past him and into the cave. "There's an asteroid on the way!"

I've got Knobby Knees Disease, but that's nothing compared to him!

Who's the Roman pointing at?

Give him knobby knees.

LINE

What's in the window?

Fill in the rest of the lab with cardboard texture.

Tinysaurus explains the **WHOLE** situation to Raptor Remedus at **TOP SPEED**. "Four drops of the magic potion on each TorPOOdo should be enough," Remedus says. "But be quick. Its effects do not last long."

"Long enough," says a passing Minidon.

Add the potion bottle.

SPARE HEADS AND STUFF

Ooh, stick a head in here.

What else is on the shelves?

Add texture to the rest of the stone shelving.

BACK AT THE TOWN HALL . . .

"I've got it! I've got it!" pants Tinysaurus.
"Four drops will make the TorPOOdoes as hard as, er,
REALLY HARD STUFF!"
"Hurrah!" cheers Ingenius. "We'll launch the
mega-hard TorPOOdoes from my catapult!"

Time has nearly run out. The asteroid **IS COMING!** Will magic Dinosaur poo flung by a giant catapult really save them all from **DOOM?**

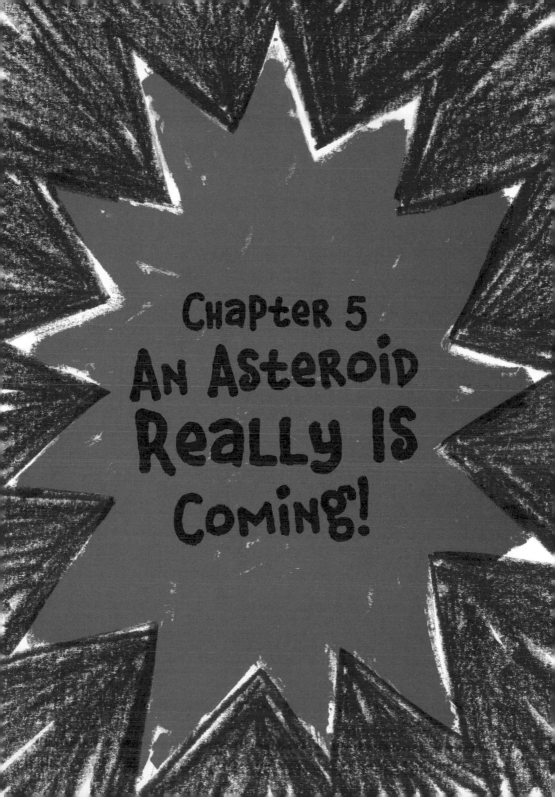

The Dinosaurs form a line, which **SNAKES** into the woods. Will they have enough toilet paper to go around? The fresh poo is then squished into TorPOOdo shapes and left out to bake in the Mars sun.

"Add the potion!" shouts Eurekadon, and the Romasaurians start dropping it onto the stinky poo bricks. **"HURRAH!"** they cheer, holding their noses.

He needs a toilet— fast!

Create a few little Dinosaurs who really have to go!

Suddenly Augustus Astronomus shouts, "It's coming!"
Lardosaurus heaves himself into the sling
("**OOF!**"), the rope is cut (**TWANG!**), and the
TorPOOdoes are flung into outer space (**KERFLUNK!**).

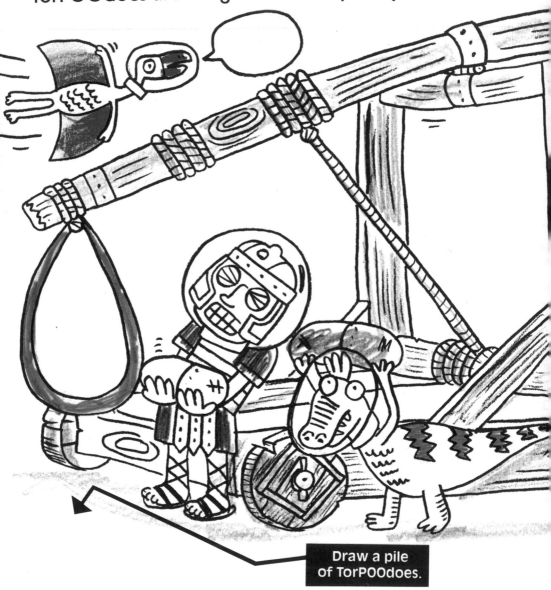

Draw a pile
of TorPOOdoes.

Draw Lardosaurus in the sling!

Add a few small Dinosaurs.

Romasauria hangs in **SUSPENSE** as everyone watches the TorPOOdoes disappear into the night sky. "If this doesn't work, we'll be **FLATTENED!**" whines the crowd. They wait, and wait . . . And then . . .

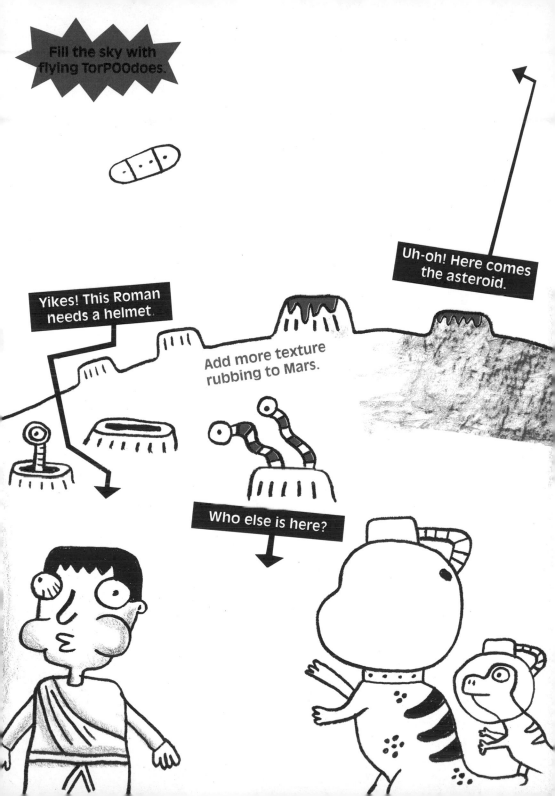

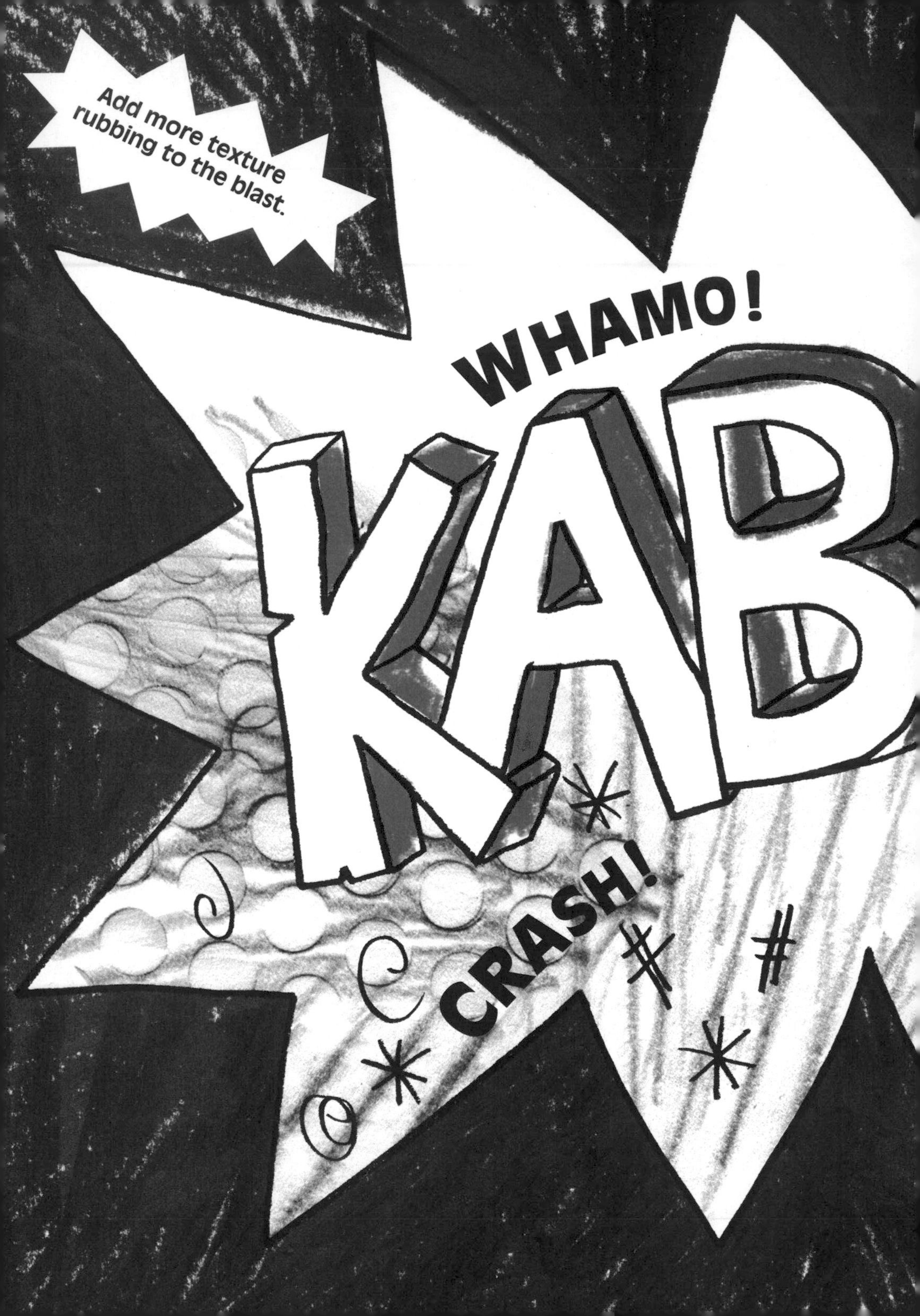
Add more texture rubbing to the blast.
WHAMO!
KAB
CRASH!

Add a smaller KABLAM and mini KABOOMS.
What other sounds do the explosions make?

A huge explosion rips through the sky, then all is quiet again — until large lumps of **MeLteD** asteroid and poo start to fall.

Add a few more lumps of TorPOOdo and asteroid.

IT WORKED!

"**HURRAH!**" the Romasaurians cheer.
"We're saved! **We're saved!** **We're saved!**"

What else is being thrown in the air to celebrate?

Now that Romasauria has been saved, the Romans and Dinosaurs decide to celebrate.
"Let's have some fun and games!"
shout Ingenius and Eurekadon.

Chapter 6
Fun and Games!

Wow! What does an angry POOgoid look like?

The first game is called "Herd the POOgoid!"
Who is brave enough to face the
Stinkiest creature on Mars?
"POOP POOP POOP!" goes the POOgoid.
The crowd goes wild!

Add small rocks and shading to texture the ground.

The crowd chants "**Cling On!**" as the next event gets under way. Who will be the first to drop into the stinky swamp-dung pit?

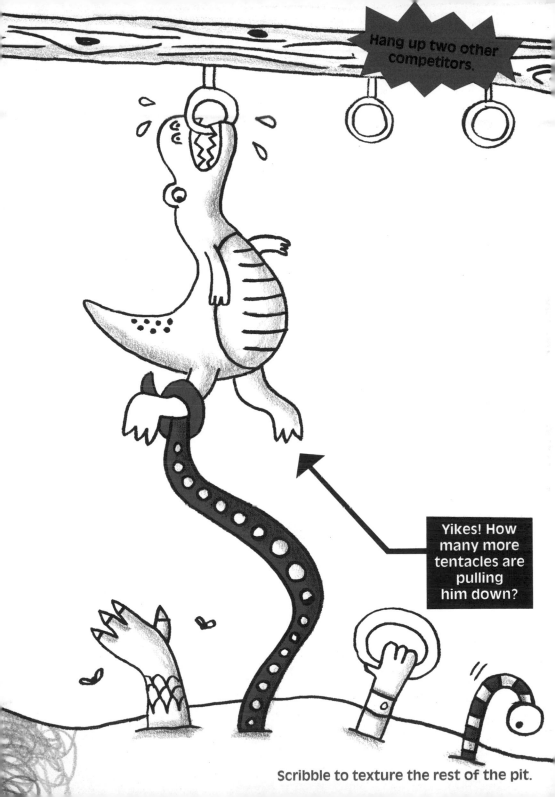

Finally, they decide to have a giant **tug-of-war**.
"**Heave**!" grunt the Dinosaurs.

What are they saying?

"**Tug**!" shout the Romans.

Finish each team!

Add more ground texture.

"Long live Romasauria!" cries the crowd, and the closing ceremony comes to an end with a brilliant TorPOOdo **SALUTE**. "Long live Romasauria!" "Can I get out of this sling now?" asks Lardosaurus wearily.

Who's the winner? You decide.

They all decide to have a feast to celebrate. The table is groaning with Roman goodies and Dinosaur treats. "Have a **ROASTED JELLIED MARTIAN GERBIL**," offers Grittus Cementus.

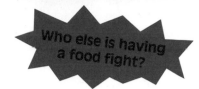
Who else is having a food fight?

Add a nice big bowl of lizard entrails!

"Don't mind if I do," says Clawdius.
"And please do try some regurgitated **LiZaRD ENtRaiLS**."
Grittus Cementus goes green and has to leave the table.

What an eventful time it's been in Romasauria!
They created a **magic potion**, invented a **TORPOODO**,
and destroyed an asteroid using a **giant catapult**!
But in the end it was all just **fun and games**!

Picture Glossary

If you get stuck or need ideas, then use these pages for reference.

If you like, you can copy the pictures. OR you can draw your own versions.

PLANETS AND COSMIC STUFF

Banana Moon

Rocky Moon

Planet Hairy

Donut Globe

Snailey's Comet

ROMAN COSTUME

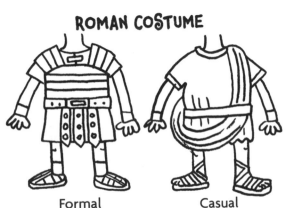
Formal

Casual

ROCKET CHARIOT

Front

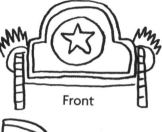
Side

MOON-COW AND FRIES

Fresh

Baked

A ROMAN AND A DINOSAUR ARGUING

TORPOODOES

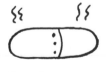
Standard

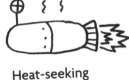
Heat-seeking

Deluxe (TP3000)

Visit our **awesome** website and get involved!

Website